I0593303

The War We Live

M. Haslem

The War We Live

Extra Copies...

To gift a friend/family member:
TheWarWeLive.com/order

Schools can order in bulk, at the link below or using
the ISBN in their own ordering system:
TheWarWeLive.com/schools
ISBN: 978-0-6452712-2-5

Dedication

This book is dedicated to those living in our modern, digital world. Victims of a "digital" war, a battle for attention, that which rages right under our noses.

Health, friendships, careers, lives and dreams... all mere collateral.

Not all is lost; hope remains. It lives amongst us, woven into our being - battered and scared, but it remains. We read, we share, we grow strong together. Written words, become our battle cry – "*squad before everything!*" - those we love most, those which too, live the same daily battle. Share this story with them - friends, family members, classmates...

For the war is fought here, within the lines of this book, and beyond the pixels of your enslavement.

This book is your weapon.
FIGHT.

M. Haslem
Share with your loved ones & help grow the army of readers: TheWarWeLive.com/share

Contents

Chapter 1 -
Different Worlds

Shoving his bullshit gift aside, I powered on my laptop. "Turn it OFF Timmy" – a children's book!? really? I'm an adult! ...well 13 now, and that's close enough.

Besides, I'm no ordinary kid - I've had to grow up FAST... I work, pay the bills, and I'm up to date with my school work, well kind of.

And yet sitting here, at the living room table, grandpa is currently millimetres from my head, bellowing his dismay into my ear...

Yea I've learnt to block him out - my trusty headphones help drown his constant complaining, as I dive into the very "evil" game he's shouting about.

"n00bSlayer13", yup that's me. Prestige level, with brand new skins... looking slick.

For me, I don't see my "screen time" as an issue. Besides, I've been a wiz at computers, phones, technology - all my life, I surely didn't see any reason to turn them "off".

"What up squad!" I shout into my mic with excitement. My friends cheer in relief, ending their anxious wait in the game lobby.

NoScopez gave me a head nod, he's my best friend, known each other since grade school.

A shove from KittenClaws, she's from the year above, a far better gamer than all of us combined, though I'd never tell her that.

"You better not miss your shots tonight" she barked, half sarcastically. "Wow!" I thought in my head, careful to not blurt it out loud.

And finally, waving in my direction, gleefully dancing, without missing a beat, was Billy... my neighbour. Placed in our team to appease his parents, he ain't the brightest, but at 9 years old, his reaction times are insane, as if he was born with controllers as hands.

I looked up, peeking over my laptop, grandpa's eyes

staring with concern from across the room. He doesn't understand — my school, my job, my friends… it's all online.

"…oh by the way, I think Timmy should keep it ON" I stubbornly whisper.

His eyes melt in sorrow, his worn wrinkly face drops in defeat to rest upon his walking stick, as the game pulls me in, and I'm submerged in my online world.

Where are my parents you may be thinking?

Nope they aren't having a night out, while grandpa babysits. This is it, this is my life, me and "Pops". It's all I've ever known.

I don't ask about my parents; besides he'd never tell – all I know is they died when I was very young.

I sometimes blame him for them not being around. I know it's wrong, and as terrible as it sounds, I wish he would just leave me alone too.

I don't need a parent; for me these pixels fill the void just fine.

What made things worst - Pops was old school, clueless in our modern world; always needing help with technology, streaming stupid stuff like football matches or rocket launches to the TV. Oh, and he haaaates computers, like no one else.

So basically that's our story, nothing special, but I'm guessing you're here because you want to know about the world collapsing on this very night?

So there I am, celebrating my birthday, just like any other ordinary, regular day...

My phone's alarm had dragged me out of bed, I'd sat through boring school, got my work done on the bus ride home, and was now set to game into the wee hours of the night.

A tiring schedule, each day moulding into the next, but hey that's life, these n00bs needed beating, killing... *slaying*, and I couldn't let the squad down.

"I'm recording, we got this" bellowed KittenClaws; she was hoping this to be our first win of the night.

Just one team remained, camped in a locked room - most likely hiding in fear, awaiting their fate.

We picked Billy up and confidently belted the door down, using him comedically as a human battering ram, the games latest feature.

The tension built, my heart raced, this is it.
"Squad before everything!", NoScopez cried out, as I pushed into the room.

My screen flickered, pixels jumped, an unbearable screeching overpowered my headphones – suddenly I'm viciously ripped from the game and in flight – hurtling across our very REAL living room.

Furniture, birthday cake, debris, and my own body, all dramatically slung off the crimson red car that had somehow violently crashed its way into my reality, straight through the front of our house.

Time seemed to stand still, as my face pressed against the car's windscreen, the drivers wide, startled eyes locked with mine, complete horror engulfing us both.

I must have passed out, after hitting the kitchens back wall - as my next memory is gazing up at my frail grandpa, somehow carrying me. Our house ablaze over his shoulder.

Surely I wasn't thinking straight, potentially from the nasty knock to my head, because in that moment, there was no one I'd rather carry me, than Pops.

Darkness came over me, and I slipped away.

Chapter 2 -
Alive and Dead

I woke to a heavenly bright light, glistering across my eyes.

Had I...? I jolted around, the crackling underneath my body distinct and instantly recognizable, I knew exactly where I was – Pops cabin. The pull-out sofa he kept wrapped in plastic to be precise.

It was here he lived, in the mountainous countryside, before coming to look after me; though I'd argue it was me looking after him.

We'd visited many times before, it's his cheap-ass excuse for a holiday. Whilst my friends all went places I could only dream about, I'd be stuck here... in this silly, tiny, wooden cabin. He seemed to like it up here, for reasons I have no idea why....

Gazing around the bright, curtainless room, my head throbbed; sounds of the accident still rattling through it, like a dying hard drive, grinding and unpleasantly loud.

Besides that though, I seemed fine, well physically at least.

Surprisingly, my trusty red, vividly bright headphones sat atop an old, drab, wooden dresser... Pops must have saved them!

These headphones were my obsession - their noise cancelling feature was my world cancelling solution; silencing the outside, while amplifying what I cared about. Not only do I wear these bad boys most of the day, I'd also bought a pair for my online character, as part of his outfit.

I checked my other vital - my phone. Oh thank God, still in my pocket.

It meant I could get some work done, but more importantly I use it for my social media and communication with my squad, for when we aren't in-game. Basically, my lifeline, for when I'm not on the laptop.

Holding it to my face, for the identity unlock, the screen remained blank, a lifeless mirror... my own tired, strained eyes gazing back. It must have turned off in the crash.

There's no reception at the cabin anyway, I figured for now, it's best to keep it off and preserve the battery.

In fact, there's no technology at all, a lightbulb is as advanced as things get up here.

I often wondered why he so stubbornly hated technology, especially when it could improve his life so much.

I got up and cautiously strolled the poorly lit narrow hall, past all the old photos of Pops with my parents, their smiles from a time before I was born.

Pops dressed smartly in them, shirts and ties; slightly hipper than he looks now. He was like a scientist or accountant back in his day.

Instinctively, I diverted my eyes to the ground, seeing the photos always made me jealous... as Pops often said, "there's a story behind every photo" ...and these were all of incredible locations, on holidays; skiing, fishing, doing stuff that made them smile and laugh.

I'd missed the ability of doing any of that with them. Even now, there's some activities I'd like to try... but hey, life is dangerous; last night reaffirmed that.

Plus let's not kid ourselves, I wouldn't know where to start.

I stumbled into the kitchen, the only other room in the cabin; it has a bed too small, a dining table propped with milk crates, and book shelves crammed towards the back. Pops was stood over the old wood stove, making coffee.

His wrinkled, well-aged face, housed eyes which always looked to hold great wisdom, stories and knowledge... sparkling blue gateways to the past. It's a deceptive trait with old people, it's just a look they have, for there's nothing I can learn from Pops.

Noticing I'd walked in, his face lit up, "Hey hey little Timmy!" he happily laughed.

How could he be joking, after all that had happened.

My name obviously isn't Timmy, and although I prefer N00bSlayer, it's actually Max.

He went on to explain, the guys car which had come off the road, right smack dab through our house, had been hijacked, no wait, "hacked"...

He'd survived, he was ok; but it wasn't just his car... everything with a computer chip seemed to have been taken over, or at least that's what Pops thought.

"Traffic lights, smart homes, the ATM where people get money out"... he irritably began listing every computer powered item.

My heart stopped in its tracks.

"TV, electrical grids, stock markets..." he continued, but I'd phased out, all I could selfishly focus on was n00bslayer13 - had he come to an end?

"Hey Max"

...no more battle royals, no more squads, my mind raced.

"MAX!" Pops interrupted, waving his walking stick to get my attention.

"We're lucky we got out in one piece, the drive up here was treacherous, if you take a look at the city..."

I flew out of the back door, scurried up the wooden ladder onto the cabins roof, which gave an amazing view of our shiny, bustling city, nestled alongside the base of the mountain.

But that's not what met my eyes, far from it - my city ominously draped in an unfamiliar cloak of dust.

Viewing our notoriously loud city, from such a distance, while surrounded by perfect silence, always felt strange - as if what we were seeing, didn't match the audio.

...but now, with our city under attack, the shocking visuals were violently mismatched, with the deafening silence.

"I'd imagine it's chaos" Pops yelled. "Just be glad we're up here, at least until things get fixed

...the important thing right now is getting more wood to heat my next coffee"

Staring down at where we lived, or should I say used to live, the daunting realisation sunk in...

I had no way to check in with my friends,
no way to do my work,
no way to do, well anything.

What the hell was I meant to do up here, in the middle of nowhere?

Slouched and defeated, I clambered off the roof and set out at finding the stupid firewood.

Chapter 3 -
An Escape

"How good is this?" Pops smugly quipped, lightly blowing his coffee; that which had been warmed, off my back-breaking work with the barbaric axe.

To me, his words were fighting words and I was seeing red. If it's war he wanted, I'd give him one.

I was already irritably tense, missing tonight's gaming session and to add fuel to the fire, I'd been run ragged all day chopping wood, as he relaxed in the cabin, carefree — reading books.

Always so gleeful, right in my face. Never upset. Yes, annoyed at my video games, but that's as down as he gets. I'd surely never seen him shed a tear. Up here, his happiness was amplified, and it was rubbing me the wrong way...

"This is some A-GRADE BULLSHIT!" I crossly snarled. I could hear him choking on his coffee in the background, as I stormed to my room, proceeding to slam the rustic door almost off its hinges.

Had I over reacted, most likely. I did half expect him to follow me in and give me a belting.

Don't get me wrong, he'd never done that before, but maybe it would be a first. He did happen to come from a generation where it was more common.

I laid there, on the pull out sofa, staring blankly into the roof. The wooden beam above, carved with numbers, letters and what was most likely names, but I could barely make them out... 'Luno'? with a love heart? It was a crazy, mashed-up chaos of all those who had stayed at the cabin, carved into history.

I was a mess, much like these carvings above. Probably if I had someone to talk to, or hang out with my own age, I'd be alright.

At least the other times I'd been here, I had company — my laptop. I'd always come prepared, with multiple batteries, to ensure everything remained charged. This time though, I had nothing, no refuge.

My mind swayed between thoughts; negative, silly, awful thoughts.

I usually avoided my emotions, brushed them aside; but out here, there wasn't much escape. I was secluded, lonely, and my mind free to attack.

My whole body felt it, not just my head. I was overwhelmed with a sense of weight, pushing down, sinking me through the old knitted quilts, into the unforgiving rough blankets below.

There were no screens to run too, no games to jump in; nothing to avoid the downward spiral.

I'm in Pops reality now, an NPC, a non-playable character, I'm just background filler to his world.

Secluded from society, in the middle of nowhere, I wondered how this fake "cabin world" was any different than that of my own pixelated online worlds.

They're both just pathways from the real world, to something else... an escape.

As if the universe was hearing my thoughts and purposely rubbing salt in the wounds... the feebly faint bulb lighting my room, proceeded to swiftly drain to nothing; intensifying my battle to hold back tears.

The old car battery used for lighting the cabin, held a measly charge... or more to the point, the vintage solar panel he used, was probably rubbish.

Either way, there was no escaping it, I was in his world now, and utterly in the dark.

Chapter 4 -
Soul Hacking

Collapsing at the mountains peak, my hike was complete - I was to be rewarded.

Laying there, cheerfully exhausted, I reached into my pocket and oh so carefully pulled out my precious phone.

My last hope, my one connection back to my life, my everything.

Being somewhat impossible to sleep, in the bright curtainless room, I'd snuck out of bed at first light, making the 2-hour journey up the mountain, all by myself.

The little cabin lay unnervingly off the grid, but up here, a bit higher, at the mountains peak, reception was possible.

And boy oh boy, was there lots I wanted to do once I got connected. Stuff I needed to do, I'd been without internet far too long.

Just thinking about the unread emails piling up, gave me anxiety. Not to mention the trove of messages going unanswered.

First on the agenda though, what mattered most - making sure my squad was alright.

This was the longest I'd gone without talking to NoScopez. We'd grown up together, combined we'd progressed our way through different games and consoles over the years. We also happened to share the same classes during the day. Hanging with him was effortless, yet enjoyable all at once.

I missed Billy making me laugh, something I hadn't done since I got up here. Whether it was his crazy game play or one of his accidental witty remarks, he was quality to have around... I guess the closest thing I had to a little brother.

And then there's KittenClaws, she was everything I looked up to and wanted to be.

Sure, she couldn't program to save herself, but her gaming skills were incredible, to the point she'd won solo cash-money tournaments. Cool and calm under pressure; in situations I'd completely freeze. I missed her immensely, in a way that was different than the other two.

Sitting on top of the mountain, thinking about each friend, fuelled my guilt; they should be up here, safe, with us. Pops should have got them on his way. Or even now, we should be going back to get them. Surely, hopefully, they were alright... down there in the attacked city.

It was time to find out...

With every hope in my being, I slide my finger over the power button, held my breath, and nervously pushed it in.

A second passed, so did another.

Finally the dead screen gloriously lit to life; in turn, breathing life into me.

I sighed with relief — things were going to be alright, I could manage this. I'll sneak up here, from time to time, contact my friends and check in with my world, from atop this mountain.

The screen grew brighter; the little pixels fed my hunger. They flickered and jarred, my brain was wiring in.

More pixel jarring... wait, hold on, somethings not right...

The screen flickered faster and faster, the pixels continued to jump, in and out of existence, and then a screeching pitch, came from within, louder and louder, rattling me to my core, to the point it was unbearable.

My face grimaced, my muscles tightened, I turned it off in defeat.

They'd not just hacked every single computer chip in existence, they'd hacked my soul.

Chapter 5 -
Drowning

A rattling anxiety pinned me down; without being able to use my phone, check my apps, play my games - I was drowning.

You might say it's foolish how reliant I'd become, but don't judge me, that's our modern world.

In fact, it's all I've ever known; born into this digital life, unlike other generations which might still be able to remember a time before smart phones, wi-fi, social media...

I had to hide my angst from Pops, I wouldn't give him the satisfaction knowing I was struggling. Drowning. A silent death.

I knew I wasn't alone in my sorrow; I'd sneak onto

the roof each night, to check the status of my battered city. Its eerie darkness, softly lit with spot fires, matched how I felt inside.

The world needs computers, I need them. They make everything easier, better, liveable.

The evidence was now clear, without processing power, we crumble.

I stumbled through those initial nightmarish days like a zombie - starved of blood, praying my phone would magically fix, that all would be right with the world.

The one upside - Pops hounding had completely gone; there was no technology that he could be wishing me off.

Besides, he was far too busy to be concerned about me, so at least I got to be alone, killing time, waiting until it was safe to head back to the city.

Of course I was bored out of my mind; kicking worn footballs to myself, hiking the mountain to try my phone and even flicking through Pop's vast, somewhat over the top, book collection.

I guess this was his version of Google; shelves and shelves of old, dusty random books and encyclopaedias, much of which I couldn't tell tops from tails of.

It's my view these books were obsolete, much like Pops.

Yea my thoughts are terrible sometimes, maybe I'm just a terrible person, but you don't understand how much he has put me through.

I glanced out the window to him sat at the end of the pier, fishing rod in hand, staring blankly into the lake. Maybe he too is killing time, bored just like me.

In all of the math & science books he owned, hand written notes scribbled throughout the margins. He must have bought them second-hand to save cash.

He never had much money; blew his savings on some big purchase I'm not allowed to ask about, and the remaining he'd lost in some global financial crisis.

He'd struggled finding and holding down a job, given his age. Occasionally he had work at the supermarket, but it's my computer programming jobs I've had since I was 8, which got us through these last few years.

Programming I found natural, as if the languages were made for me; I understood them, and the computers understood me.

Hence my excitement to see a few random books related to programming, on one of his shelves. If I couldn't be on a computer, I could at least read about them.

I worked my way through John Backus' Fortran Manual, an old programming language I'd wanted to learn, but never had the time.

I read an inspiring book on Alan Turing, who used his computer science skills, to crack "Enigma" a cipher messaging device, which helped win a war and save thousands of lives.

And finally, an extremely old, vintage looking book, I literally had to blow dust off, just to reveal its name, "Scientific Memoirs... Oct 1843"

Well worn, falling apart at the seams; I turned the delicate pages with extreme caution, attempting in vein to keep it together.

Detailed in it, the first computer, a steam-powered "Analytical Engine" by Charles Babbage; and his assistant's thoughts on it - Ada Lovelace, the first ever computer programmer.

She wrote... "The Analytical Engine can do whatever we know how, to order it to perform."

I liked that, to me it meant limitless capabilities... it just comes down to us.

An old photo had fallen from that very page, as if it was being used as a bookmark.

In it, Pops pictured with 3 others, all cheering and high fiving... quite possibly the happiest I've ever seen him. On the back, penned in faded ink, "Margaret, Charles, Gene & Bob – 1969"

Bob being my grandpa; maybe this was his squad, from when he was younger!

Seeing it made me sad — my own squad was constantly on my mind... how were they doing? Were they ok?

Yea most likely cars didn't burst through their damn houses, but I imagined things being quite bad for them in the city... I had no way of knowing, and it was driving me nuts.

If I could, I'd swap with them, in a flash. I'd much rather be dealing with the unsafe city, and instead have them up here, bored out of their minds. Strangely enough, they'd probably handle it here better than me, like it was a novelty or some kind of weird adventure.

No matter what the situation, I seemed to always

want to be in their shoes.

Growing up, I envied them, each and every one. In fact, all the kids at my school I'd happily trade places with, even Billy.

Their parents, despite being lame and comically dorky, were just one generation removed from their children. They at least had a chance to bond, to somewhat relate.

Pops and I were multiple generations apart,
he wasn't made to be my parent,
and I wasn't made to be his son.

Chapter 6 -
Last Hike

I knew how stupid hanging over a cliff was, yet I didn't think twice; to me, it was a necessary risk.

Yelling out of frustration, my broken phone had popped clumsily from my hands, bounced along the ground, only to mockingly disappear over the mountains edge, onto a small ridge below.

Putting more faith than one should ever place in a dead, rotten, dried out tree, I hung dangerously from it, desperately reaching for my useless phone. My vulnerable life in nature's hands, and one questionable branch.

Mere millimetres away, just a bit more... I loosened my grip, to lengthen my stretch. Swiftly I slipped and begun plummeting to my fate.

A befitting way to die, for me at least, chasing the very technology, that had controlled and somewhat prevented me from truly living in the first place.

There were no reset buttons, no do overs... my stomach sunk faster than my body, in a spiral race downwards.

In that instant, freefalling to the ground, regret was all I felt. So much I'd wanted to do, but had held back. My life was to be over, before it'd really begun.

My body impacted with the ground, in an almighty thud.

I cried out, overwhelmed with immense pain, as wild waves of soreness rippled through my back. My own cries, a relief to hear... I was alive!

I'd fallen a good 4 metres; crisp fresh autumn leaves catching me, saving me from tumbling further down.

Gazing up in agony, my phone still on the ledge, it remained in sight; my mind went back to planning. I can probably reach up, climb a bit, and get it from below.

I felt the stern gaze, the heavy breathing... I was in

trouble. I swung around, expecting to see Pops. In every way, I wish it had been him.

Shades of wonderful browns, soft, plush, cuddly... a great, majestic, mad as hell... BEAR!

Fierce eyes of anger stared into me, teeth glistening from its grumbling mouth, radiating a deep unnerving sound, that which reverberated all through-out my body.

He'd probably watched my entire phone rescue mission, or maybe to him, I was just an intruder that had fallen from the sky...

Either way, I'd crashed into his world and he was mad as hell for it.

My heart, having not beaten since the fall, was now loudly pounding like a drum in my chest. A steady, solid, rhythmic fear.

What on the earth had I gotten myself into.

"Be big, act tough" I remembered some survival video I'd seen on the internet, as I slowly pushed myself out of the leaves, to stand.

As if he was mimicking my moves, the bear gracefully straightened upwards, rising on powerfully thick hind legs; his height many multiples of mine.

Towering over my weak, typical gamer stature, there was zero chance I was going to start beating my chest and staring him down. Nor was I going to stand there, and pretend I was a tree either. I knew my decision. RUN!

I shot off, like a rocket, my body almost beating my brain with the idea. Down the mountain I blitzed, in a frantic combination of running, tumbling & sliding.

I expected he'd be gaining, I knew they were quick, but heck, I wasn't going to glance back to check, I was blazing.

A solid, moss-laced tree abruptly put an end to my discombobulated escape; I'd travelled about 80 metres from where I'd started.

Glancing up the mountain, the bear to my surprise, had just stood there; watched my entire clumsy struggle.

Maybe he was just happy to scare me off, or more likely, he was too smart to attempt the awkward dash I'd just performed.

Gasping for air, my eyes locked intently on the bear, I slowly backed away, down the mountain, fearfully on all fours.

Adding distance between myself and the threat, until it was out of sight.

What a rush! I'd never felt anything like that; and very much never wanted to again.

Needless to say, I wouldn't be going on more hikes anytime soon. I was glad to be returning to the cabin. The safe, apocalyptic proof, bear-free cabin.

Nature had kicked my ass today. Losing my phone seemed insignificant to the fall I'd survived and the bear I'd escaped.

Arriving back, I staggered in the direction of the cabin, for a lay down, for a rest, and maybe even a cry.

Pops was at the end of the pier; carefree, happily fishing. His mood was to change, as he glanced my way ...

He would be stressed about how long I was gone. He'd notice I was covered in dirt. He'd lecture me for not being safe...

He smiled, and waved in my direction.
I awkwardly waved back, as if all was fine.

And that was it, he hadn't even noticed I was gone!

Didn't bat an eye, nor say a word.

I decided I wouldn't tell him. I knew everything about Pops, but what happened this afternoon, I'd keep to myself.

This secret was mine, and mine alone.

Chapter 7 -
Born Again

I wore my headphones, even though they weren't plugged in, just so he knew I wasn't there to chat.

Still a tad shaken from the whole bear thing yesterday, I'd followed Pops down the pier, out of boredom, to observe him fish.

To me it seemed stupid, just sitting there, waiting for a bite, but heck, I literally had nothing else to do, I may as well embrace the boredom, ironically lean into it.

The calm, tranquil lake, was a perfect mirror; the sky, the clouds, even the faint moon vividly reflected in the water, as if there were two incredible skies.

Pops sat there, his legs dangling off the pier, staring deeply into the lake.

I sat there, even more bored than him, watching him watch the lake.

The pier was unlike those in our city, no concrete in sight, no dirty waste water flowing below. Instead... well aged, cracked, faded wood, along with wobbly planks. It looked weak in appearance, but it felt comfortably strong to be on, as if it had stood there forever.

Time passed differently, sitting next to pops, looking out over the lake; like everything was slowed down, forced to match it's extreme calmness.

Eventually Pops caught a fish, and I hate to say it, but yea it was cool to see; watching his eyes light up, reeling it in, taking the hook out, placing the fish in the box...

I took mental notes of everything he'd done to catch that fish, or at least what I'd noticed - it didn't seem too difficult at all.

Later that day, I decided, I had nothing to lose - I inquisitively requested having a go on the fishing rod.

Of course I'd fished before - in video games, but I

daren't give him that potent fuel to ridicule me.

Now I don't know if he'd trained the fish to bite or I just got lucky, but within what felt like only a few minutes, I was jolted into action.

The line suddenly snapped tight, water splashed and Pops talked me through slowly, calmly, reeling in my first catch!

It was a beautiful, tremendous fish, with amazing glittery scales. Pops even took a picture of me holding it, using his archaic Polaroid camera; one which captured and developed the photos on the spot. He handed me the picture to keep...

Initially, it looked like a blank piece of paper, but as I held it, I watched it slowly develop before my eyes, turning from nothing, into a photo of me stood there, end of the pier, holding that fish, with a big smile. I don't remember smiling, but there it was, captured in the picture. A bit dorky, but I liked it.

Sure I had lots of photos, but nothing of me doing anything like this, and none I could hold, physically. Mine were all just pixels on a screen, stored on a drive. This however was in my hand, no power required to view it, it was old school and it was awesome. Yea, I probably wouldn't be hanging it up, but I'd surely keep it in my room, to look at.

That night, under Pops guidance, I cooked the fish, which to my surprise, and maybe even his, tasted amazing! No supermarket, no packaging, no reliance on anyone else, it was 100% caught, and cooked, all by me.

The following day, I rushed down the pier and started at it, before him. Attaching the bait, casting the line, staring out blankly.

Hilariously I had it down pat, and surprisingly found myself able to get through the days a bit easier, just by trying some of the stuff Pops was up to.

A new found energy was starting to carrying me along and at night I would collapse with joy at how much we had accomplished.

Fishing was only the beginning; Pops begun teaching me how to build shelters, how to hunt, how to protect myself, how to survive, and I guess, how to "live".

Well live in his world at least.

We were so different, yet out here, absurdly, we were now starting to get along like a house on fire.

Ah yea, I really shouldn't use that analogy any more, it saddens me to think what we left behind, but at the same time, this new life isn't too bad.

Living like Pops, was opening my world, just in different ways.

My morning alarm on my phone was now replaced with the sun, my video games replaced with real life adventures, n00bslayer replaced with... me.

We must have been away about 2 weeks, maybe more, maybe less. Crazy thing, I had no way of knowing, nor did I care.

All I knew was, the longer I was away - the more I loved this new life.

I was reborn again - Max.

Chapter 8 -
Trapped

"Wait for it, wait for it..." Pops pleaded.

The branches straining under the weight, little bits of bark already breaking away, falling softly from the tree.

"Not yet..." he continued.

My heart raced, sweat rolled down my face.

"Ok NOW!" Grandpa shrieked at the top of his lungs, a sound I will never forget.

I heaved as hard as I could, clenching the rope with all my strength.

Just when I thought it hadn't worked, the crackling of the tree branch roared out, the giant cage shot down, rocketing into the earth, sending a shock wave through my bones and dust into the air.

We had trapped our first rabbit! With thoughtful planning, a bit of bait and a whole lot of luck, we'd actually got one.

The dust settled, revealing a tiny, little creature, brown and cuddly, happily sitting... alive of course! Our trap wasn't designed to injure him, just capture him.

Pops was ecstatic; looking over at his enthralled face, I couldn't help but smile.

This was a side of Pops I was unfamiliar with. To be honest, it was like hanging out with a different person, a complete stranger.

Sure, back in the day we had fun, but all that was a distant memory, faint and hard to see; this however was bringing things back - a fun, confident, positive Pops. The Pops that now stood before me.

It wasn't so much catching the rabbit that excited me; like let's be honest, what was I going to do with a rabbit... sitting there, in the cage, all cute — I definitely wasn't going to be killing it.

It was seeing Pops though, filled with joy, which I was strangely liking. His happiness was now rubbing off on me, and I selfishly enjoyed it.

Observing his eyes full of glee, it was at this point, I haphazardly blurted out "sorry".

Completely out of nowhere, even catching myself off guard, I had said sorry, and there was no going back.

His face slowly crimpled up in confusion. I stumbled through apologizing for ignoring him so much over the years;

"it's just that… my life 'IS' computers, or at least was. Until we got up here, I couldn't get out, I was tra…"

"It's in your blood Max" he cut me off to explain, which made no sense, in fact, it didn't explain anything!

"I've got something to show you, when we get back…" he insisted mysteriously.

Much to my relief, we let the rabbit go, as it was just practice. However, it was somewhat reassuring, if we ever ran out of tinned food or fresh fish, and we absolutely had no other choice… we wouldn't go hungry.

On returning, he took a crow bar and used it to

crack open an old wooden shed, that which had remained sealed, off limits to me since forever.

He had a few sheds, which stored tractors, canoes, work areas, but this one, from a young age, this is the ONE that was strictly out of bounds. This was his "adults shed", not for kids like me.

Toggling a dusty switch, the room softly illuminated, under a flickering, weak light.

Pops paced around, proudly pulling sheet after sheet away, revealing the unthinkable.

Chapter 9 -
Bloodlines

Huge metal like boxes; maybe they were cupboards, with dials, rotors and and…

Realization struck; I began darting across the room in disbelief. My mind now racing as fast as my feet, analysing what he'd just uncovered.

The biggest, most ancient looking mainframe computers I could ever imagine.

The solid, attention grabbing machines ranged in heights between those equal to my own… about 5 foot, to ones much larger than Pops.

Each of them, elegantly ageing in an off-white metal, coupled with striking-red panelling, timelessly exuberating the vibrance of their past.

"I haven't been in here for quite some time", Pops reflectively remarked, admiring them alongside me.

"Hold on" still in total disbelief, "these are all computers?"

"It's just one Max. An IBM System 360 - Model 91" he said in a technical, almost excited-geeky tone, that which I hadn't heard from Pop's before.

"This thing is just ONE computer! It takes up the whole shed... it's frickin huuuuge! I bet it's crazy powerful..."

He bemusedly agreed, "well, at the time it was"

There was so much to take in, my eyes didn't know where to focus, nor did my brain know what to think.

An actual computer, here at the cabin, all this time! More than that, it'd potentially been here my entire life... Was I dreaming? My computer hating Pops, just happens to have the biggest damn ass computer I've ever seen, and I had no idea about it. This couldn't be real...

Pops interrupted my thoughts -

"Although you've been fortunate to live a relatively safe childhood, there is ONE thing, I utterly fear for you Max"

It was something I'd heard him say a thousand times before, but for the first time in my life, gazing at the majestic computer, I was listening...

"That one thing I fear, can wage war on us personally - steal our time, our health, our lives..."

"Evil programming" he termed it.

"For you and millions like you, living in our modern world, this is the war we live..."

I intently took it in, he continued "most programmers are good natured; creating software to benefit others...

But over the years, I watched many programmers get lead astray; chasing profit and power over people's health, enslaving their time... that in part turned me off computers."

I guess it somewhat helped explain his anger towards my obsessions.

I felt horrible, I was maybe, definitely, possibly... a victim of this "evil" programming.

I changed the subject, anxious to know more about his cool ancient computer.

"So what did you use it for pop? Did you use it to slay n00bs like I do?" I probed in excitement, the thought of Pops being a gamer tickled my mind.

"Well, not quite" he chuckled, "we put a man on the moon."

"No way!" I blurted out, in brazen disbelief.

He had to be joking. I stood there, like a deer in the headlights, blinking my eyes like an idiot.

"Long before you were ever born, I worked for NASA, this is one of the machines we used... I too was a programmer Max"

The shock was instant, as if my brain had been blown straight out the back of my head.

"I like to think your wizardry on the computer is by no accident. Yes, I worry about your screen time, but you must not lose sight... you're a programmer Max ...it's in your blood" he remarked with a tone of ancestral proudness.

I tried to process what he was implying,
I felt joyous, but now conflicted.

I don't need computers anymore, he probably should stop calling me a programmer. Up here, it was no longer an interest to me.

"It's your background Max, the skills you've had since a kid, that's why you're made for this" he said with excited, wide eyes.

By now, I was completely dumbfounded, made for what? What was he going on about?

"Ma-Ma-Made for what?" I stuttered out.

"We need to get you ready…. it's time we do some GOOD programming" he enthusiastically quipped.

"We?"

Pops dramatically pulled a lever, a generator grunted and puffed itself to life, loud sounds of electricity filled the air, and the machine came alive.

Dials turned and clacked, hundreds of tiny little lights beautifully blinked, tapes wound… my knees buckled, my senses overwhelmed and my mind short circuited, into a euphoric dazed state.

It was an amazing sight, but I had to ask…

"Why are you always needing help with technology stuff, if you know how to run all of this?"

Pops smiled, effortlessly bypassing my question, "let

me get you up to speed with it" he insisted, tapping the computer with his walking stick.

"As you know, everything with a modern microprocessor was taken over, this computer seems to be untouched because of its older technology."

I watched in ore as my grandpa fed data into the machine, processed answers, and attempted to teach me certain parts.

I thought I had decent programming skills, but this gave me insight into everything, how it all worked on the ground level.

That night Pops joined me, sitting on the roof, staring at our city. Though to be honest, his eyes more focused on the stars above.

The single, well-worn solar panel, provided the perfect back rest to lean against, as we talked.

I felt stupid not knowing he'd worked for NASA. I wouldn't say he hide it from me, but he definitely hadn't bought it up, and I guess I missed the signs.

Having shared his secret, I thought it was only fair to spill the beans about the giant grizzly bear I encountered. The story I told, had him expressing a wide range of emotions; being nervous, laughing and showing genuine excitement, as if he was almost proud of me.

I looked down at the plumes of smoke, rising from our dying city, perfectly illuminated under the full moon.

"What's our plan Pops?" I nervously asked.

Pops happiness changed to concern, a face so grieved it was uncomfortable being in its presence.

"I need you to learn quickly" he sternly insisted, with a clear degree of impatience.

"If authorities haven't fixed what's going on down there, I'm thinking, with this computer, maybe we can help"

I wasn't going to question his delusional thought process, if he wanted me to learn this ancient machine, I would do so, to keep him happy.

As long as I could continue on with the new exciting stuff he'd been teaching.

Chapter 10 -
Fish, Code, Sleep

Dawn would break with my line being cast, sending out the first ripples through the pristinely calm lake.

Followed by a full day wrestling with the massive machine. Learning the ins and outs, its quirks, its pitfalls; trying to absorb all the knowledge Pops was rapidly, almost hastily dishing out.

A few outdoor activities peppered in, throughout the day, then back to sleep, to happily do it all over again.

An endless enthusiasm had ignited within me — I could think clearer, learn faster, and was actually excited about getting up in the mornings —I'd awoken from a life, I didn't know I was sleeping through.

My hunger to learn - fuelled by the realization Pops cared for me, evidently more than I'd ever known. We'd rarely seen eye to eye, but I was starting to understand, maybe he did just want the best for me.

"See how these two vacuum columns in the 2404 hold a steady excess of tape?" I nodded, I wouldn't admit it to him, but in some ways, I was thrilled to be his protégé.

He continued "This excess tape is what allows for the rapid reading and writing speeds, without putting sudden direct tension on the tape"

The gravity of what was happening, did not go over my head. Yes, he was just my boring, old, negative, stern Pops... but at the same time, learning from someone who had helped us get to the moon, and learning on the very computer they'd used, felt historically epic.

It's strange to think, without him and his team pushing technology forwards... my life would've been drastically different.

I could never imagine accomplishing something as massive for mankind, as he'd done.

Under his guidance, I enthusiastically typed, each keystroke boldly stamping physical holes into paper punch cards, ready to be fed in and stored by the giant IBM 2404 tape units.

Smells of oil pleasantly wafted about, a subtle reminder the electronic machine was just as much mechanical - with many moving parts.

Characters were encoded in 8-bits, we had compiled Fortran, my new favourite language, beyond that, I'll admit, I knew very little. Well compared to Pops that was.

For him, it was like riding a bike; his actions operating on muscle memory alone... procedures, lessons and error handling he'd learnt, over and over, back in the 60's.

I was energetically chasing him around, watching, asking and learning from all he was doing. Similar to how I'd observed him catch the fish, this just happened to have a million more steps, buttons and lights...

It was fascinating, and not just because I'm a geek! Purely from a history standpoint, learning the old machine, seeing how the technology had progressed, from this room sized computer, up to the devices I take for granted today - it was like having a time machine.

A glimpse into the past, a peak into a time, before I

existed, to a time when Pops was young. His excitement operating it, had him reliving his youth and I was along for the ride.

The basics of the computer were shockingly similar to our new ones, just of course, all blown out into huge dimensions, and a lot of it was manual.

It was as if we were inside the computer, vital clogs in its operation, part of the machine.

We weren't just inserting code and expecting instant responses, but instead actively taking part in the computer processing.

The level of control and freedom was like nothing else.

No other programs vowing for my attention, no distractions pulling me from my work.

I was free to experiment, to process, to learn.

It was programming, in its pure form, and I was alive again.

Chapter 11 -
Guidance from Above

A fierce beauty radiated, in all directions; the hills, the lake, the water... pixel perfect. The depth, the colours, the detail, and we were amongst it, rendering our way effortlessly through the ripples!

Pops up front, me behind, mirroring his moves, paddles in sync.

It was my first time in a canoe... as the electronic devices I'd usually choose, over the risk of drowning, were no longer an option. I gotta say though, I wasn't regretting it one bit.

We'd probably set out a tad late, Pops had spent the entire afternoon crawling around – rewiring some of the thick cables and replacing transistors… general maintenance, in case we were to be taking the computer into the city.

Gliding effortlessly, the lake provided little to no resistance to our forward motion, nor to our conversation… out here, it felt like I could ask Pops anything. There was a calmness that was not only contagious, but hard-coded into the atmosphere.

"Is it normal for the machine to need so much work?" I enquired, from my position in the back of the canoe.

"It sure is… that's why I've got so many spare parts, it's been like that since 1968"

"Things have improved a lot since then, right?" I remarked, trying to think back to when my laptop last carked it.

"I reckon we've gone backwards Max. Your new phone, has what… just a slightly better camera than your last? Unless we're pushing technology forwards, aggressively, to the point things are breaking, then we're going backwards…

Getting to the moon required aggressive leaps in technology, unconstrained by the current thinking of the time."

An interesting take Pops had, his generation being superior with its speed in developing tech. To be fair, they were literally shooting for the stars… a more audacious goal, than improving phones, to make a sale.

To my surprise, Pops had twisted his body, a complete 180, to stare me directly in the face.

"Don't be constrained by current technology" he pleaded at me.

A strange request, especially with all the 'current technology' being down, but I remarked "sure"

I think he was having a moment. Talking about his past… the NASA stuff, seemed to dissolve his shields, revealing a deeper somewhat more emotional side.

With the pier no longer in sight, darkness was setting in. The sun had gone down some time ago, and we were far away, on the wrong side of the lake.

We probably should've begun heading back, but I was keen to keep going, plus I was no longer wobbly, like at the start - clinging to the pier, rocking the canoe, desperately trying not to capsize… there may have been some squealing too, but let's not focus on that.

We rowed over to observe a paddle steamboat, laid in ruins, a relic of the past. A big white and green, double story vessel, though it was shipwrecked or whatever the term is for steamboats no longer in use.

By now the darkness was concerning "Are we going to be ok Pops? Visibility is dropping…"

The moon was lighting the surrounding water, but that's about it. I could no longer make out the mountains and the shoreline had completely vanished, like a 'low-quality' setting in a video game, rendering distant items out of sight.

"The moon" Pops replied.

"Yea it's providing some light" I agreed,
"…but I can't see far"

"No Max" …he'd stopped paddling and was leaning back, gazing upwards. I followed suit, staring at the brightly lit surface - the little crisp details, unlike its drab look, when viewed from the city.

Though honestly, it may have just been my well-rested eyes - seeing clearer, recovered from the strains of my past life.

"For thousands of years, our ancestors have looked

to the sky, to know where they are, and to guide them to where they want to go" he said, in one of his reflective tones.

"You can tell where the pier is, from the moon?" I asked.

"Well not exactly, but I've got a rough idea"

The ripples shimmered with the moons light, providing a perfect glowing bed for us to glide, towards our destination, guided by above, as man had apparently done for ever.

Men have been also getting lost forever too, so I wasn't hanging my hopes on it.

Sure enough though, we weren't far off. It seems the past had steered us back, and now, apparently, it was up to me to guide the future, or something along those lines, according to Pops.

It's best to not think about things too deeply

...I'm a kid and just had my first canoe ride, I was stoked!

Chapter 12 -
Mission Above All Else

The "FEED STOP" light blinked a hot red,
the IBM was down and Pops was going to kill me.

Nervously, I checked the tape drive, but nothing, no
data being fed in.

Oh boy, I'd messed up something massive. Why did
he leave me running it, all by myself?

I'd destroyed not just his dinosaur computer, but his
delusional dream… I would be accused of ruining his
wacky ideas of saving our city.

The machine growled and clacked in anger, I
worried it might be overheating. Clueless and out of

my depth, I grabbed a bucket of water, swung back and...

Oh I shouldn't... I hesitated, water will surely make things worse. I put the bucket down, clearly I couldn't think straight.

How this machine ever got us to the moon, is beyond me. It was running smoothly all morning, yet now, as soon as Pops steps away, I end up in a hot mess with it.

The door burst open and grandpa limped in, catching me succumb to a pile of stress.

"What's going on!?" he inquired.

I stood their blank faced, and braced myself for his stern yelling.

"Umm no data, feed stop, punch card reader..." I trailed off mumbling in confusion.

"Ahhh the old Card Muncher!" he injected with a calm excitement of nostalgia.

"Card Muncher is what we used to call the Card Reader..."

Still frantic, I raced over and just as Pops had surmised, one of the cards in the reader had jammed.

"I just rip it out to unjam it?" I nervously asked. "Spot on Max, it jams often" he said with confidence.

Examining the strewed-up card, I figured it was best to not mention I'd put it in backwards.

"How did you stay so calm Pops?" I queried, fascinated that his manner had been so vastly different than mine.

"Has your school not taught you about the Apollo missions?" he asked, already knowing to well the answer to that.

After a moment of reflection, he said...

"Our missions had many issues. The key was NOT to panic... not everything goes to plan, in fact, it's to be expected... improvise and continue on with the mission, that's the most important thing —

Mission above all else" he said with a level of proudness, still somewhat strange hearing from him.

"With that final lesson, I think we're ready" he concluded, "we'll be leaving in the morning"

I was starting to get the hang of it for sure, but I desperately insisted I needed more time.

 "Pops, there is so much left for me to learn, I don't think I'm ready... plus what if something happens to you?" I cringed at the mere thought, no way would I let anything happen to Pops.

"We can't risk waiting any longer, people are potentially suffering" he politely stressed. "Besides, I'm 97, I've lived a good life, helping others is more important to me"

"And if I'm not ready?" I probed again.

"I can assure you, if or when the time comes, you will be ready"

Chapter 13 -
Fuelling Our Return

Doorbell chimes filled the air, mixing with the smell of fuel. Maybe I should have left the jerrycan outside...

I think he knew I'd siphoned the last drops from the truck — I had to, to keep the generator running. At least this way, our big city trip had been put back a day.

Pops had made his way to the counter, standing there, ready to pay for the petrol. It was obvious there was no one in the store to serve us, but it didn't seem to fuss him - he'd wait.

It had taken an hour to get here, walking from the cabin. This gas station all that remained of the old, tiny town – this and a rundown motel next door. Frozen in time. No complex electronics, no technology... no smoke clouds or chaos either.

Sunlight filtered through the shutters, splayed across the otherwise dim store; dust particles dancing in each beam of light.

While Pops waited, I took the time to browse the products left to age: expired candy bars, a pair of broken sunglasses and magazines. I didn't have to read the date on the PC-MAG I'd picked up, the beige thick computer 'screamed' 1990's.

"Holy cow, why hello Bob!" I almost hit the roof, unaccustomed to hearing other voices as of late.

A man had pushed himself through the discoloured, plastic door curtains, and was heading right for Pops.

Bushy-grey beard, blue overalls, and a white shirt, that which only amplified the dirt and grease, laced and worn into his attire.

Pops laughed, putting his hand out to shake. Having none of that, the man used it to pull him in for a giant hug.

The reacquainting, looked like a scene from an old painting, the two of them perfectly drawn in a gas station of their era. What looked out of place, was me - standing there in my dark hoodie.

Pops pointed in my direction, bringing more attention than I'm comfortable with. "Walt this is Max, my grandson"

The old man walked up and gave me a nudge. For some damn reason, people seemed to greet me by checking how strong my footing was.

"You like that magazine, take it" he said with a smile. I politely put the magazine back.

Walt turned to Pops, "How's everything holding up?"

"Yea, things are not too bad, considering"

I couldn't believe what I was hearing. Our house destroyed, technology under attack, and to Pops - "not too bad"

"Winters almost here, are you planning on bunkering down in that cabin of yours?"

"Nah, we're currently working on something"

Walt smirked, "That doesn't surprise me. And Alice?"

The mood instantly changed, as Pops slumped his shoulder and shook his head, "fair while back now"

Walt nodded, changing the subject "So just the gas?"

He moseyed on behind the counter, to the ornate, metal cash register. It's wooden keys, not too dissimilar to that of a computer. Flying his fist downwards, he gave it a good thud and it flew open, with a satisfying chime.

Walt reached in and pulled out curious piece of brown paper, marking a line into it, I presume next to my Grandpas name.

Now obviously I hadn't expected Pops to whip out plastic and start tapping and swiping, especially with the power being down, but I hadn't seen this coming either — a tally system! Mates keeping track of who owed what... older than cards or paper money...

Just as quickly as it'd opened, he shoved the register closed. "Done" he laughed.

I waited outside, while they talked a bit more. My muscles strained, the jerrycan significantly heavier, now filled.

I dreaded the walk back. Not because it was going to be more difficult, but because it was getting us closer to our city trip. Our trip into the unknown.

Chapter 14 -
Carved in Wood

Metal cracked & strained under the sheer weight of the monstrous computer, precariously positioned atop the old farm trailer.

We were fuelled up, almost set to head back to the city - an exciting, yet overwhelmingly fearful thought.

What would we be returning too? Had our house been saved? Were my friend's ok?

And Pops question I'd rather not even contemplate... would we be needed to help solve whatever was going on...

According to him, we potentially had the only uncompromised computer power in the world.

To find a machine this old, completely in tack, along with a programmer old enough to know how to use it, was apparently rare.

If this computer, slow as a potato, is humanities last chance, we're toast.

I finished packing the last items - a small icebox, which held today's catch, and Pops old camera, just in case.

Pops was busy rushing around, throwing together last-minute boxes of cables, tapes, punch cards and all types of spare parts for the computer.

I strolled through the cabin one last time, checking if we'd missed anything. A few extra pokes of the fire, like I'd done on my previous lap, to extinguish my paranoia just a bit more.

The fire poker, prodded me with an idea. I marched off in the direction of my bedroom, down the little hall, hot metal stick in hand. Climbing up onto the sofa, standing at full stretch, I began etching my name into the cabin, into the chaotic mess... half carved, half burnt in – "MAX"

A few items sat on the dresser I'd overlooked - my headphones and the photo of me with the fish. I didn't need the headphones, but, then again…. if our city trip absurdly became a like "mission", similar to those in my video games... begrudgingly, I put them around my neck.

"Let's go!" echoed down the hall, along with a few car horns... Pops had started the truck. On my way out, I thumbtacked the picture to the hallway wall; added in amongst the vast sea of family photos, now sat my own.

We set off, winding our way down the mountain, ever so slowly, heading cautiously in the direction of our city. The roads travelled, apocalyptic ghost towns; the inhabitants, long gone.

It was my job to keep an eye on the computer, in case it came loose or the trailer began to break in some way.

Turning the dial, each channel - crackling. No voices, no music, nothing but radio silence. I looked at Pops, "that's not good"

He shrugged, unphased, focused purely on his driving.

"I enjoyed the cabin", I had to fill the dead air with something... "I felt relaxed there"

"That's freedom Max - that's what the cabin is. One day, that cabin will be yours"

Not knowing what to say, I just nodded and smiled.
Like it'd be pretty cool, but I couldn't see myself
living there... it's more of a holiday house.

Crossing our cities large, beautiful bridge,
untouched from the happenings on the ground, the
tension built, we were almost home.

Forgetting my job from time to time, I glanced back.
Still there, the huge computer, in all its glory.
Museum grade technology, rolling through our
newly vacated, technology free suburb – had it
potentially regained its title of 'world's fastest
computer?'

Nervously peering out, as we pulled into our eerily-
quiet street, the smell of our house abruptly filled
my lungs, choking me with sadness.

Burnt, dry charcoal, where the house used lay.

I rushed up to what was left of the front door, able
to see completely through to our backyard.
Everything I'd ever known, my entire life, reduced to
a crisp.

The hacked car, still amongst the rubble; crimson
red no more – paint melted, its bare metal carcass
all which remained.

Pops rested his hand on my shoulder, to comfort

me. Or maybe just to make sure I didn't run into the ruins.

Strange thing, the longer I stood there, the weirder I felt... I should have been sadder than I was, I should have been crying... I just couldn't stop thinking of the positives though, all that had changed, over the past few weeks.

A little sparkle of colour caught my eye, in the drab burnt out mess. It was a note, a flamboyantly bright note, dramatically knifed into the side of our chimney.

A message! "City tower building, somethings up, we are going there - SQUAD BEFORE EVERYTHING"

Alive! I was filled with joy. My friends must be ok. Let's not fret about how old the note might be, in this instant, things were looking up. Not only that, but it sounded like they were actively trying to get things fixed.

There's no tighter, closer group of people, we'd literally shared thousands of hours, our knowledge of each other tactics, strengths and weaknesses...

If anyone stood a chance, it was us.
I grasped onto that false hope with all my might.

Chapter 15 -
Barrier Gone

My mood was swiftly quashed, coming face to face with what our city, under computer attack, looked like up close.

Bleak. Soulless. Its heart removed.

Observing it from afar, from the cabins roof, didn't quite do it justice, but being in amongst my dying city, awoken the nightmare.

Driving through the streets, the sounds of sirens reverberated through the air, filling any possible calm silence, with a continual hellish note.

Traffic lights flashed. Shops lay ransacked, looted & unapologetically torched.

I barely noticed at first, but people, everywhere!

Saddened, worried people - blending in with the carnage, as battered as their weary city.

Viewing from the passenger window, as we drove along, was like watching little scenes, viral clips playing out, short stories of other people's lives...

A middle-aged man, running frantically with a watermelon under his arm... a group of angry young men, armed with sticks and various sporting equipment... two kids, roughly my age, viciously fighting each other, using just their bare fists... and in amongst it all, a lonesome, saddened young girl, no older than 5, sitting on the ground, staring at our car whizzing by, staring at me, the viewer. The guilt-ridden viewer. Shielded by the cabin, protected by Pops, their struggle I knew not of, their hell I had not shared.

Arriving at the tower building, we came to a complete stop, in front of the basement entry. Pops was very cautious negotiating the intersections, as they were all out of order.

A lady stood on the corner, hugging her cat, shouting loudly in our direction. Her hair and overall look - crazy and untamed, her eyes filled with desperation.

I slightly leaned out to hear. Was she warning us? Maybe she needed help?

"No no", grandpa asserted, winding up my window, as to protect me from the unknown.

That wasn't going to stop me - I flung open the door and jumped out. Besides, she looked harmless.

"Are you ok?" I shouted cautiously.

She scurried over, onto the road towards me, her eyes fixated on my clothes, my fresh clean clothes.

"I'm searching for cat food, but the shops have been looted"

Ah relief, "No worries!" I said calmly, walking over to the icebox. I pulled out two fresh fish.

"I caught them myself" I proudly proclaimed.

Her eyes lit up, and so did her cats. She thanked me, over and over.

See Pops, I thought, no reason to be alarmed.

"Get back in the car" he yelled once again from behind me, the anger in his voice the usual tone when met with my defiance.

I smiled and waved her a good day, turning back towards the car.

A bone trembling thud filled my body, as a truck whizzed by my back, standing my hairs individually on end, brushing my shirt and ripping my headphones right off my neck... spinning me in circles.

My trusty headphones, my barrier between my world and the outside world, gone.

I looked to where the old lady and her cat had stood moments ago.

My stomach sunk in an instant; the truck had destroyed them. Wiped them out. Slayed them.

I collapsed in guilt. Grandpa grabbed me and threw me into the car, like the misbehaved rag doll I was.

Gasping for air; mortified, traumatised and angry all at once.

Was that my fault? What immense evil had we come back to?

We pulled into the basement. The pristine, clean & unscarred basement, marred by my squeals of shock.

If whatever is happening to our city, our country, our world, was potentially happening from this building, I was going to stop it, before anyone else got hurt.

Revenge is not a good trait, but right now, it's all I felt, and I was roaring to act on it.

Chapter 16 -
Squad

Distraught and running on adrenaline, I rushed with helping load the computer off the trailer, into all four lifts.

The buildings electricity was unaffected by the attacks – promising for us, as we needed to power the computer, in a location that wouldn't be seen.

Elevator music seemed to bypass my rattled brain, singing directly to my soul. A nice, almost familiar song… its tune, striking distant notes of my childhood.

Glancing at Pops, his smiling face looked to be holding back tears. Simultaneously happy and sad, as if his expression couldn't make up its mind.

I rushed over and threw my arm around him, "are

you alright Pops?"

"Yea… I am now. You should try to meet up with your friends, I'll get this all connected" Pops said assuringly, hitting the buttons marked "ROOF" in each lift.

He disappeared into the last lift to close, his smile and mind a million miles away.

Still shaken, thinking about the cat lady, I found myself unnervingly alone. Skittishly, I took the stairs. If my squad is here, I knew where I'd find them. Just one flight up, I pushed the door open, and entered the lobby.

A familiar cheer filled the room - the entire squad, in real life! I joined in the boisterous celebration, ecstatic to see they were ok.

NoScopez was already nodding, I nodded back with a grin, as I begun flying backwards.

A real life shove from KittenClaws, my head smacked into the wall behind me, amazing!

And of course, Billy, who was happily dancing and waving in my direction.

"Looks like you've seen a ghost, are you ok?" KittenClaws analysing my face with a level of concern.

"Yea you could say that. I'll be fine though... are we all ok doing this?"

"We are if you are n00bslayer!" Billy shouted.

"It's Max now" I corrected him.

"Ok um... Max", NoScopez happily mocked.

"We've been here a few days" KittenClaws explained, "the issue is, the penthouse seems blocked off, we can't open the doors, and we are certain, seeing this building is untouched..."

"Yup, whoever is doing this, is on that level", NoScopez interjected.

After psyching ourselves up, and talking through some tactics, we piled into the lift, pressing level 54... the penthouse.

"Look guys, I've bought someone to help" I cautiously admitted to them, correctly expecting some backlash.

"But we're a squad of 4, what do you mean?" Billy's hesitance shared amongst the group.

"We're going to need all the help we can get" I

urged, they grudgingly agreed.

The lift doors opened, and we were met with Pops crawling along the ground, with a computer cable in his mouth.

You bought your grandpa?! NoScopez blurted. Looks of utter confusion washed over them, as they all pulled the same eyebrow raised face.

This was the very grandpa they'd listened to me complain about, almost on a daily basis, for years.

The lift doors closed.

"Omg, can we just get out of the lift"... I hit the button, the doors opened again and we filed out.

"Look grandpa is our hidden weapon"
I insisted.

Pops jumped up proudly, to address my 3 friends...

"Hey little Timmy monsters!" he looked them over, one by one. Oh great, grandpa's about to belittle my squad, not cool.

"Focus everyone! Grandpa is a legend at old computers... we bought one with us, it's unaffected by the attack... right now it's all we've got"

Pops handed me the cable he'd had in his mouth, and the ancient looking control terminal he'd ripped from the machine.

"You couldn't do wireless? Bluetooth?"

He stared back at me, without batting an eye.

"Never mind, thanks, this will do"

"The big computer is on the roof, just above" he touted, addressing the squad, "I've written a small program that analyses and can send short commands to devices, within the building"

"Wow, impressive" I turned to the team, "you see this is how we fight back!"

I anxiously typed some code, sending a packet to the first device address it had found. Allowing for a slight delay with the old technology, I knew it wouldn't be instant, but this seemed ridiculous. I sent another, and another.

An uneasy silence came over the room, as everyone anxiously waited to see if we could control any devices.

"Give it time" I assured my nervous looking team members.

As I spoke, the floor lamp next to them flicked ON... then OFF.

Collectively, all our eyes whipped around, focused intently on the lamp.

Boom, it lit back up, shining a barrage of bright, wonderful, hope bearing light.

"Ohhh great, we can control a lamp" KittenClaws uttered sarcastically.

"Well, we're dead", Billy laughed.

"Yup that's it for us", NoScopez joined in.

"It'll hopefully do" grandpa insisted.
"I'll head back up, and lower a new cable down, into that locked room.

But please wait for me, before attempting to get in, it could be dangerous..."

Chapter 17 -
The Face of Evil

We walked the spacious hallway, its exuberant walls draped in evil. Black & white photos of programmers lined each side; softly lit, like a spiritual shrine.

My gut sunk the further down the hall we walked. I guess on the upside, they all looked scrawny in the photos, like a decent gust of wind would blow them over. If things were to get physical, given my new survival training, maybe we stood a chance.

Arriving at the end of the hall, the ominous locked door. Its carved, ornate wood, the final barrier between us and the evil.

We pressed our ears up against it; though it wasn't necessary, clear loud laughter could be heard coming from the other side.

We had dealt with locked doors before... in-game. Without waiting for Pops, we picked Billy up and proceeded to use his feet as a human battering ram.

It surely wasn't seamless, but after the 5th hit, the lock buckled, and the door swung open... revealing our nightmare.

The blazing city, combined with glowing computer screens, softly lit the most villainous, evil programmer one could ever imagine.

Dramatically outlined, perfectly casting his shadow over us, his suit arced and zapped with electricity.

Little dust particles dramatically snowed down, softly from the ceiling above, igniting into tiny beautiful sparks, on contact with the man's suit.

His hands guided his controller, his body twisted and turned with purpose. Large wires ran into his suit, he was plugged in, controlling not a game, but the world.

"Squad before everything" NoScopez whispered to us, as we entered. The level of fear in his words, an unusual addition.

"Is this the villain we're looking for, or are we after a different villain?" Billy asked sarcastically with a grin.

"Very funny, keep it down" I insisted, though relieved he was breaking up some of the tension.

Approaching nervously, the man was completely clueless to our entry; he was like me when I'm in-game, submerged in another world.

Lucky for us, besides not hearing our entry, his VR goggles also blinded him seeing the fresh cable Pops had lowered from a crack in the roof, now dangling uncomfortably close to his head.

NoScopez stretched up, carefully grabbing the cable, which was connected to the vintage computer, sitting on the roof directly above.

I plugged it into my terminal, and we were ready.

Without hesitating, I reached out, and desperately wrenched the villains goggles from his head.

He was taken back, jolted into our reality.
His shocked, wide eyes, staring into mine.

"Nooo" grandpa shouted, bursting in, realizing we hadn't waited for him.

"It's about time" the man menacingly chuckled, abruptly shooting across the room, knocking helpless Pops to the floor.

My blood boiled, seeing someone physically attack my Pops; what kind of sick person was this.

My squad leaped into life, as I stood there stunned, blood boiling but frozen in place.

Billy jumped on his back, while NoScopez and KittenClaws jostled to get the controller from his clasp.

With no time to waste, my body, like a laggy computer, finally finished booting up, I'd gotten my act together and rushed in, only to be met with a stray punch to the face.

I wobbled there dazed, blood dripping softly from above my eye.

"Just program Max!" Pops cried out.

He had a point, time to use my skills. With the old terminal under my arm, I dashed across the room, and slide towards Pops, the strong tethered cable bringing me to an abrupt stop, next to him.

"We'll be ok Pops, I got this", my zero confidence coming through clear as day, in the crackling of my voice.

I smeared away my blood, which had dripped on the keys, and began typing.

My neural pathways flowed and vibed with the 1960's technology, I was wired in to history, and fighting for our future.

The evil programmer raised his controller; his electric suit now hummed and buzzed with unnerving arcing sounds.

Grabbing at my team mates, one by one, he sent dramatically violent, uncomfortably bright bolts of electricity, hurtling into them, painfully contracting their muscles, immobilizing them to the ground.

Turning his sights towards me, I noticed him approaching in the corner of my eye. My squad laid paralysed wincing in pain, Pops injured - all helpless watching what was to happen.

I frantically sped up my typing. Each keystroke, a desperate step towards saving all that would come, powered by the learnings of all those who had come before me.

I closed my eyes, and my fingers raced with the combined knowledge of every good programmer...

Ada, Backus, Turing, Pops and the entire Apollo team.

I was a mere vessel for them, housing & out pouring all of their ideas, knowledge and wisdom, into beautiful, elegant, perfect code.

The man's footsteps came to a rest in front of me. His suit began howling, powering up. I was to be zapped.

I fumbled over the last 3 lines of code, unclear if I'd made any mistakes and desperately struck ENTER.

Nothing. I proceeded to open my eyes. Even if it had worked, the delay was going to be our downfall.

I gazed up in utter fear, his finger now looming towards the zap button on his controller.

He pressed it. That was it.

The tiny electrical pulse, rocketed down, into the building's fibre optic cables, now travelling at the speed of light, up into his control pack... the electrons from the ancient machine, beating the press from his controller, short circuiting his electrical suit, zapping him to the ground with a thud.

A cheer erupted - we'd done it!

All the games we'd played, hours upon hours spent together, even the training from Pops, it had all paid off.

NoScopez proceeding to smash the man's controller... with him no longer in power, the hacked systems would begin to restore.

I helped everyone to their feet. KittenClaws threw her arms around me and we began chanting "squad before everything!" Pops took a group photo, capturing us celebrating.

In that moment, I was the happiest I'd ever been, all of us were. We had played our part towards restoring the world.

"I'm proud of you", Pops cheerfully admitted; immense relief washing over me, hearing such words he'd never spoken. I gave him a massive hug, things had never been so perfect.

He geekily began diagnosing our now fixed world... "The issue wasn't programming itself, it was the human corruption and the centrally controlled nature of these systems. There's a way of stopping this in the future - trustless, decentralized, peer..."

I laughed, agreeing it sounded interesting, but after all that, I never wanted to program again.

Technology might hold all the answers,
but the real world was for me.

And boy did I look forward to getting back to the cabin. Sitting on that pier. Relaxing, without a care in the world.

How woefully wrong I was...

Chapter 18 -
No Code Left

A little niggling sound, barely noticeable. Was it just in my head? I tried to ignore it, but it grew louder, unnervingly louder — laughter.

Vial, sick laughter.

It combined with a clacking beat; the drum of high heels impending on our location.

The increasing sounds, wiped our celebrations, replacing them with fear, installed directly into our cores. I felt my muscles tighten, bracing for what was to come.

The door aggressively swung open, and standing there was a lady, decked out in a flaming red, triple breasted suit and transparent AR goggles, like some kind of super villain from the future - with an obscure taste for 1980's fashion.

She was connected, but wirelessly, with full vision of both worlds.

She lifted the evil man up into a chair. He was content in watching what was about to happen, and something told me this woman was going to put on quite the show.

"Did you really think you could out program us?" she laughed, in a slightly demeaning tone.

Pops turned to me and sympathetically whispered, "I'm sorry Max"

My face crimpled up, what did he have to be sorry about. Whatever it was, I took it that he was conceiving defeat.

I nodded, in agreement, it was over. If he believes we're doomed, then we are; at least we'd tried.

My left ear filled with a giant gasping sound. I turned to Pops, his mouth wide open, sucking in air, as if he was trying to muster energy, that which I knew he had none left.

To my astonishment though, he jumped up, wielding his walking stick, like a weapon.

I'd never seen him move like this - with youth, with purpose, with confidence. He spun, ducked and weaved - wiping the woman's legs out from underneath her.

Seizing the opportunity, my squad rushed in, tying up the still half-paralysed man, in case he begun to recover.

The lady, with Pops towering over her, reached out, towards the air in front, pressing a button... a button that wasn't visible in our reality, but in her vision, it clearly existed - with horrendous consequences.

The ground violently shook underneath us, glass exploding out from the window, flying in all directions, showering the room in little vicious shards.

We all fell over, except Billy, he'd manage to dance his feet fast enough to stay upright.

I tucked myself into a ball, bracing for impact, was the building coming down?

Dust slowly cleared, thanks to a roaring wind, gusting through the now glassless window frame. The room vulnerably opened to natural elements & crisp unobstructed sounds of our dying city.

Two levels of red flashed on screens behind her -

she'd blown out the bottom floors!

She was far above and beyond being an "evil" or "bad" programmer... this lady was the devil.

Body trembling, I glanced at the demanding cursor, still there on my screen. More code was once again urgently required. I couldn't repeat what I'd done, for starters she wasn't wearing an electrical tethered suit.

She got up, Pops swung his walking stick again, but this time, she caught it one handed, mid-flight.

My squad ran at her, but aggressively, one by one, with her free arm, she knocked them flying.

For once, we were woefully out matched, we were the n00bs in this. We were to be slayed.

Pops continued to struggle in vain, but she overpowered, pressing him against the wall, using his walking stick.

With my squad shaken, and huddled behind me and Pops being squeezed, it was again down to me and my code.

I held my breath, as I began to output lines like a blur. Programming without knowing the exact end in sight, desperately trying to reach a destination unknown.

"You never could control your programming"
grandpa whispered in pain.

Even under attack and with me trying my best, Pops
was having a go at me. His way of pressuring me,
only rattled my chain of thought.

I looked up in anger, expecting to see his concerned
eyes staring me down, but instead they were deeply
focused on the lady.

He was staring HER down, just like he does when
I've misbehaved… he wasn't talking to me at all!

In that instant, my world tore apart, my heart
shattered into a thousand pieces, and I was laid
bare.

Everything was clear, but jarringly muddled. Shock
engulfed my body, paralysing every nerve, organ &
thought. My cursor blinked, but my heart had
stopped.

"It's ok… everything is ok now" she remarked at me.
"We've done this all for you"

Her eyes were wild, blue and large, her
demeanour… defiant.

My rattled, crumbling brain strained to think. I looked out the blown window, our city on fire… my actual world, out of control.

"We reign over it all Max… have so for years. Us and other programmers" the lady gloated.

The lady who had just used my name. It couldn't be, they couldn't be.

"You're delusional Luna! Leave him out of this" Pops grunted, from his position pressed against the wall.

"She's quite the opposite" the evil man snarled from his chair, feverishly working at untying himself.

"She's parented him, we both have, much better that you ever could! All from afar, keeping him safe, keeping him on the screen"

The lady chimed in, "we parented everyone, how people live, think, socialize; we just took it to another level"

"We knew doing this would get you here Bob, this was the only way" the man asserted.

"And well, now you're here to see it… this is pay back!", she cheered, raising her arm, and pressing another nightmare riddled air button.

Soul thumping explosions, one after another, roared through the empty window. Dust balls rising up, along our beautiful city bridge, and then just like that, it dreadfully began crumbling into the water. Its deafeningly collapse, filling my heart with fear.

I looked down at the terminal, I had to desperately code something, FAST!

Something to defend bridges? To stop her code? To stop my, my… mum. I couldn't think.

These WEREN'T my parents, no way! Familiar maybe in looks only… to me, Pops was my father, and nothing would change this.

Grandpa, looked over at me forlorn, "You know what to do!"

He was reaching his arms upwards, at the cable coming from the roof directly above him. I think he wanted to code, or was trying to tell me to get coding.

I smeared more blood from my keyboard. Evil, vial, impossible to clean off blood. Their DNA in me - I felt it, pumping through my veins. Grimacing, I fought the idea, I refused to accept it.

I glanced at my terminal, clueless. The cursor anxiously blinking, but I had no code to action.

The computer had failed me. There was no answer to this.

She pressed another, life destroying air button; live footage of an entire building crumbling filled the screens behind her. The red pixels oozing with death.

She was determined to cause as much chaos, damage & loss of life as possible... all across the globe.

Each button pressed, lives gone, families ruined, and me helpless to it all.

My skills had hit a brick wall, the war was lost.

Grandpa's grip weakened, a solitary tear ran down his exhausted face, as she proceeded to squeeze the remaining life from him with one arm, and hold the rest of the world's lives in the other.

The evil man, now free, stumbled to his feet, walked over to Pops, and shockingly joined in, helping to drive the walking stick into Pop's throat.

She raised her deadly arm again.

I had nothing.
We'd lost.

"NOW!!" Pops shrieked, with one final breath, unnervingly familiar.

Oh god, I knew what it meant.
What that shriek meant.

Tears flooded down my face, as my body took over, as if I was watching my own awful actions, as a shocked bystander.

I yanked the terminals cable as hard as I could, with all my strength.

Nothing. Once more.

Her finger extending to the air button...

Just when I thought it wasn't going to happen, the sudden, unbearably loud sound of the roof cracking roared out.

The full weight of technology that got us to the moon, rocketing down through the buckling roof, crushing my world, sending shock waves through my heart.

A thick cloud of dust instantly filled the air, where Pops had fought.

"Mission above all else" I wept to myself, gazing into

the thick cloud of hell.

My Pops, my everything, gone.

I'd accomplished something not many can say they
have... I'd done my part for humanity.

The world was saved,
and I was utterly alone.

Enjoy this book?

Thank you for reading *The War We Live*!
As a new author, reviews help immensely. Honest reviews, no matter how small, are much appreciated.

If you've enjoyed this book, I would be grateful if you could spend just 3-4 minutes leaving a review. The links to do so are here:

TheWarWeLive.com/reviews

Share with your friends:

If you think your friends and family would also enjoy the book, please share it with them:

TheWarWeLive.com/share

Study material for schools:

Teachers looking to add *The War We Live* into their curriculum or suggested reading list, can download questionnaires for students, based on their level of schooling.

Questionnaires & bulk discounts available here:

TheWarWeLive.com/schools

Is this the end for Max?

The generational adventure continues for Max... and maybe even his <u>grandpa</u>! Enter the competition to **win a copy of the next book:**

<u>TheWarWeLive.com/competition</u>